CAPTAIN FACT
CREEPY-CRAWLY
ADVENTURE

**Read all the adventures
starring the fact-astic**

CAPTAIN FACT
CREEPY-CRAWLY ADVENTURE

by
Knife & Packer

VOLO

Hyperion Books for Children
New York

First published in the United Kingdom by Egmont Books Limited, London
Text and illustrations copyright © 2004 by Knife and Packer
Volo® is a registered trademark of Disney Enterprises, Inc.

Printed in the United States of America
First U.S. edition, 2005
1 3 5 7 9 10 8 6 4 2

This book is set in 13/19 Excelsior.
ISBN 0-7868-5573-8
Visit www.hyperionbooksforchildren.com

CONTENTS

STARR

CLIFF THORNHILL
TV'S WORST WEATHERMAN

PUDDLES
THE ONLY
WEATHERDOG ON TV

CAPTAIN FACT
THE WORLD'S FIRST
INFORMATION SUPERHERO

KNOWLEDGE
CAPTAIN FACT'S
FAITHFUL SIDEKICK

NG . . . .

LUCY
HEAD OF MAKEUP AND CLIFF'S BEST FRIEND

THE BOSS
HE'S SCARY!

PROFESSOR MINUSCULE
HEAD OF THE FACT CAVE AND THE BRAINS BEHIND THE MISSIONS

FACTORELLA
PROFESSOR MINUSCULE'S DAUGHTER AND ALL-AROUND WHIZ KID

CHAPTER 1

PRESIDENT IN PERIL

It was a boiling hot summer day. TV's worst weatherman, Cliff Thornhill, and his copresenter, Puddles the dog, were enjoying the annual office picnic.

Well, they would have been enjoying the day if it hadn't been for all the annoying insects around. And the fact that Cliff had gotten the weather forecast wrong—again.

WELL, I FORECAST RAIN.

"Look at this, Puddles," moaned Cliff. "There's flies in the sodas, wasps on the desserts. . . ."

"And I've got *ants* all over my apple pie–flavored dog biscuits!" Puddles exclaimed.

While Cliff, Puddles, and the rest of the office were struggling to fight off the local wildlife, there was one person who was

having a great time . . . the Boss. He had put up a personal mosquito net, which meant there were no creepy-crawlies on him *or* on his table, which was groaning with treats. With a chocolate éclair in each hand, he was happily dancing to his favorite song in a bug-free environment.

Suddenly, the music stopped.

"Oh my gosh!" yelled the Boss. "This is the biggest news story in decades! Everyone, back to the studio. We need to create the best news coverage ever! I'll be there as soon as I've finished my doughnut, strawberry cheesecake, banana split, chocolate-chip cookies, fudge sundae. . . ." The Boss's voice trailed off. He stuffed one of his éclairs in his mouth.

"Do you think the president is going to be okay?" asked Lucy. Lucy was Cliff's friend from the Makeup department. They talked as they headed back to the studio.

"I'm sure he's being taken care of by the best doctors in the world," said Cliff.

"Where are you going?" asked Lucy. Cliff was not heading in the right direction. "Aren't you going to watch the newspeople prepare the story?"

"Um, no," gulped Cliff as he opened the door to his office. "We've got to, er, start preparing tonight's weather forecast. I think it's going to be, er, hot tomorrow." With that, he slammed his door shut.

That's strange, thought Lucy. There's another crisis, and Cliff and Puddles have disappeared again. And why were they wearing raincoats? It's beautiful outside.

As soon as Cliff had shut the office door he threw off his raincoat and looked down at Puddles. Then he exclaimed:

THIS IS A MISSION FOR CAPTAIN FACT!

And Puddles pulled down the secret lever to reveal the entrance to the Fact Cave.

FACT CAVE

CAPTAIN FACT

KNOWLEDGE

"Knowledge," huffed Captain Fact as they ran down the corridors of the Fact Cave. "If we're going to save the president, we're going to have to find out what bit him—and quickly. When we've pinpointed the creepy-crawly responsible for this horrible crime we will be able to identify the cure. And it's not going to be easy. **KER-FACT!** There are over one million different species of insects!"

"But how bad can a creepy-crawly bite really be?" asked Knowledge. "I'm always getting bitten by bugs on my walks. A few scratches and a couple of biscuits and I feel fine." Whenever Puddles turned into Knowledge, he was able to talk.

"Some creepy-crawlies are a lot more dangerous than others," said Captain Fact. "And the dangerous ones have all kinds of weapons at their disposal." Just then his knees began to knock as he felt the stirrings of a . . .

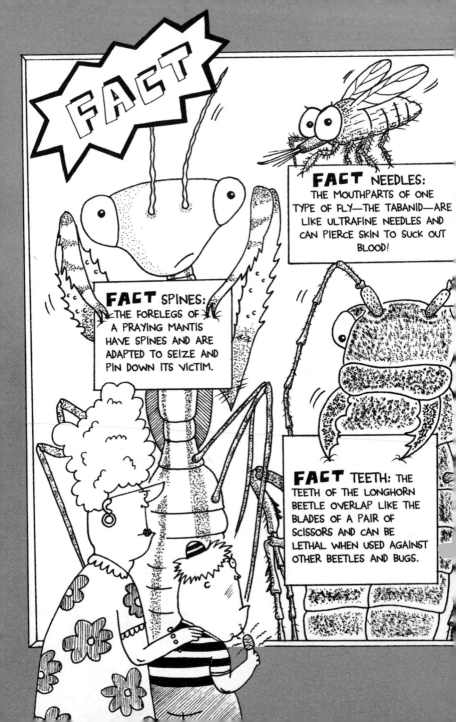

"Those are serious bugs!" Knowledge said nervously.

"You're right, and unfortunately, we're going to have to get up close and personal with a whole world of these crawlers, if we're going to save the president," said Captain Fact. Just then the door to the Nerve Center opened.

CHAPTER 2

THAT SHRINKING FEELING

"**A**h, hello, Captain Fact and Knowledge. What kept you two?" asked Professor Minuscule, the world's shortest genius. "The president's condition is not good. The creepy-crawly bite has affected his brain. At first, he was twitching and mumbling. Now he's barking in a high-pitched manner, sort of like a Chihuahua. You have to start searching for the creepy-crawly responsible for this as soon as possible."

"Well, then, let's get going!" said Knowledge as he tried to swat a bug that was creeping in the direction of Professor Minuscule's lunch. "But first, let me just get this bug."

"STOP!" screamed Professor Minuscule. "That's not a bug, that's Factorella!"

"Factorella?" said Captain Fact. "But she's so tiny."

"Of course she is. I shrank her," said Professor Minuscule, "with . . . my latest invention, the Shrinkotron 2000. And I'm going to shrink you, too, so you can investigate creepy-crawlies from a bug's-eye view."

Taking careful aim at the mini Factorella, Professor Minuscule looked down the viewfinder of the Shrinkotron 2000 and squeezed the trigger. There was a big bang, a flash of blue light, and then, standing before them, was Factorella—as her normal-size self.

"Dad! Why did you unshrink me?" asked Factorella. "I thought I was going on the mission."

"Factorella, you know you're not old

enough to go on missions," Professor
Minuscule said sternly. "You've still got
years of superhero training ahead of you.
Plus, we might need you if there's an
emergency. Now, what's Factotum got for
us on creepy-crawlies?"

Factorella heaved a big sigh and sat
down in front of the control panel of
Factotum, the Fact Cave supercomputer. A
screen popped up full of buggy facts. . . .

THE SCIENTIFIC NAME FOR CREEPY-CRAWLIES IS ARTHROPODS. SOME THAT YOU MAY ENCOUNTER ON YOUR MISSION ARE:

INSECTS: THEY HAVE SIX LEGS, THREE BODY PARTS (HEAD, THORAX, AND ABDOMEN), AND ANTENNAE, AND MOST HAVE WINGS. EXAMPLES: BEETLES, GRASSHOPPERS, AND FLIES.

MYRIAPODS: THESE CREATURES HAVE LONG, SEGMENTED BODIES AND *LOTS* OF LEGS. EXAMPLES: CENTIPEDES AND MILLIPEDES.

ARACHNIDS: THERE ARE HUNDREDS OF THOUSANDS OF SPECIES OF ARACHNIDS. THEY ARE CHARACTERIZED BY FOUR PAIRS OF LEGS AND NO WINGS OR ANTENNAE. EXAMPLES: SPIDERS, SCORPIONS, TICKS, AND MITES.

"Now that you have a better idea of what you will be facing, it's time to be shrunk!" exclaimed Professor Minuscule. He took aim with the Shrinkotron.

"Don't we have to prepare for tonight's weather forecast?" Knowledge asked. "It's going to be a tricky forecast, what with the barometric—"

Before he could even finish his sentence, Professor Minuscule had pulled the trigger of the Shrinkotron 2000. There was a loud bang and a flash of blue light. In seconds, Captain Fact and Knowledge had been shrunk down to bug size.

"Don't step on them, Factorella!"
warned Professor Minuscule. He carefully
picked up the shrunken superheroes.

Addressing the tiny twosome, he said,
"You're probably wondering how you're
going to get around. But you have no need
to worry! I've got another astonishing
invention to help you."

Then, Professor Minuscule fished around in his lab-coat pocket and produced a matchbox.

"Your astonishing invention is a matchbox?" asked Captain Fact.

"There aren't even wheels on it," said Knowledge.

"Please! Give me more credit," said Professor Minuscule, as he opened the matchbox. "Behold—the Insectopod! It's an all-terrain, jet-powered, submersible, miniature machine, and it's smaller than a cornflake!"

24

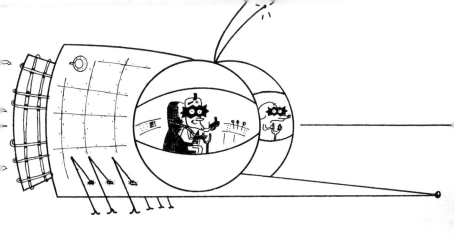

As Captain Fact and Knowledge strapped themselves into the Insectopod and prepared for takeoff, Professor Minuscule's voice crackled through the intercom.

"I'm still trying to piece together what the president did during the day—*crackle*—he's too incoherent to tell the doctors exactly when he got bitten—*fizz*—some creepy-crawly bites are slow-acting, so the bite could have happened at any point during the day—*whirr*—however, we do know he woke up feeling itchy—*crackle*—so your first stop is the presidential bedroom."

With no time to lose, Captain Fact fired up the Insectopod and buzzed out of the Fact Cave.

SECRET FACT!

HOW DID PROFESSOR MINUSCULE BECOME THE WORLD'S SMALLEST GENIUS?

NOW . . . BACK TO THE ADVENTURE.

CHAPTER 3

BEDBUGS
BITE BACK

As Captain Fact and Knowledge whizzed along in their Insectopod, they got closer to their first stop.

"Look, Knowledge. The president's house," said Captain Fact. "Security is going be tighter than ever."

As they flew over the heavily guarded compound, Knowledge had an idea. "The president has a pet cat called Fangleberry," he said, "and, as we say in the dog world, 'Where there's a cat, there's a cat door. . . .'"

Sure enough, Captain Fact soon spotted a cat door and steered the Insectopod through the unguarded entrance.

Barely avoiding a swipe from Fangleberry's paw, the Insectopod buzzed up the stairs toward the living quarters.

"Well, that was a close call. We have no time to waste with cats. First stop, the president's bedroom," said Captain Fact as they zipped through the keyhole.

"I just saw something move in the bed," Knowledge said nervously.

"Let's check it out," replied Captain Fact.

After carefully landing the Insectopod on the bedside table, Captain Fact and Knowledge slid onto the bed.

"Oh, isn't that cute," said Knowledge. "A family of orange bugs sleeping by the president's teddy bear."

Suddenly, the antenna of one of the orange bugs twitched.

"I think we woke them up," said Captain Fact nervously. "**KER-FACT!** Bugs' antennae are used to detect vibrations and smells."

"*I* don't smell," protested Knowledge.

"Well, smelling shouldn't be your biggest worry. Those are bedbugs, Knowledge."

"So?" asked Knowledge.

"So . . . they live on blood! Run!" cried Captain Fact. The two superheroes sprinted back to the Insectopod.

Once they were safely back inside the Insectopod, Captain Fact and Knowledge headed for the president's kitchen.

"Bedbugs can give you a nasty nibble, which is enough to make the president itch, but wouldn't affect his brain," explained Captain Fact. "The kitchen is probably swarming with creepy-crawlies. Maybe we'll find our assailant in there.

"First thing we have to do is find the grossest part of the kitchen," Captain Fact continued.

"That's easy—underneath the fridge," said Knowledge. "It's amazing what you find down there."

Captain Fact and Knowledge nervously crept under the gigantic fridge.

"I feel like we're being watched," said Knowledge.

"I think we are," said Captain Fact, as they slowly became aware of dozens of

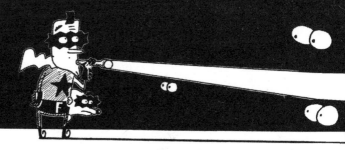

pairs of beady eyes staring at them . . . and an awful scuttling noise.

"RUN!" screamed Knowledge.

"There's no need to run," said Captain Fact. "I think it's just a bunch of harmless cockroaches." Then his ears began to wobble as he felt the start of another . . .

"Wow! I had no idea cockroaches were so amazing!" Knowledge exclaimed.

"And the most amazing part for us is that they aren't deadly," said Captain Fact as they got back in the Insectopod.

"So why are they trying to climb aboard?" asked Knowledge, nodding at the

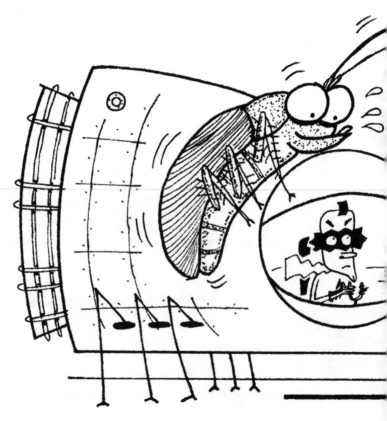

large group of cockroaches salivating over
the windscreen.

"I think they smell your biscuits,"
Captain Fact said.

"Well, they're pepperoni-flavored,"
explained Knowledge.

Suddenly, Professor Minuscule's voice crackled through on the intercom. "Cut out the chitchat—*crackle*—I've just found out that the president always takes a pre-breakfast walk in the palace garden—*fizz*—investigate at once—*crackle*—things have gotten worse. The president is now juggling doughnuts and balancing a goldfish bowl on his head. . . ."

With the professor's suggestion to go on, Captain Fact steered the Insectopod back through the cat door and out into the presidential garden.

CHAPTER 4

BUZZ OFF!

As Captain Fact and Knowledge flew over flower beds and the lawn, they couldn't believe how many creepy-crawlies were out and about.

"This place is bug central," said Captain Fact. "It's only when you're this teeny that you realize just how many insects there are. Let's check out those daisies and see what we find."

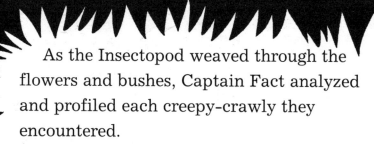

As the Insectopod weaved through the flowers and bushes, Captain Fact analyzed and profiled each creepy-crawly they encountered.

KER-FACT!
LADYBUGS UNDER ATTACK LET OFF A SMELLY FLUID.

KER-FACT!
A BEE'S WING BEATS 11,400 TIMES A MINUTE.

KER-FACT!
THERE CAN BE OVER TWO MILLION EARTHWORMS IN ABOUT 2.5 ACRES OF EARTH.

KER-FACT!

EARWIGS GOT THEIR NAME
BECAUSE PEOPLE BELIEVED
THEY WOULD CRAWL INTO
YOUR EAR WHEN YOU WERE
ASLEEP AND BORE INTO
YOUR BRAIN.

KER-FACT!

STAG BEETLES AREN'T
VERY GOOD AT FLYING
AND SOMETIMES HAVE
TO MAKE CRASH
LANDINGS.

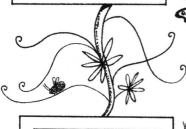

KER-FACT!

SLUGS ARE GREAT
CLIMBERS AND CAN
CLIMB UP TO
ALMOST 30 FEET!

"So none of these bugs could have bitten the president," Knowledge said disappointedly. "I knew we weren't going to find anything dangerous in the flowers."

"Don't be so sure, Knowledge," said Captain Fact. "If we're going to find our creepy-crawly, we're going to have to think like a creepy-crawly. Now, if you were the kind of poisonous creepy-crawly who'd bite a president, where would you hide out?"

"On the swings," Knowledge suggested. "They're fun and a little dangerous—for a bug."

"Don't be silly," said Captain Fact. "If you were a nasty, poisonous bug, you'd be lurking in the deepest, darkest, dingiest, most hidden place you could find. . . ."

And with that he steered the Insectopod down into an old hollow tree in the very furthest and most overgrown corner of the president's garden.

They hovered, looking around 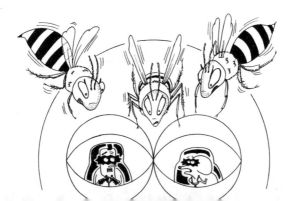 the dark and gloomy area.

"There's nothing here," said Knowledge with a sigh of relief, "except for a few wood lice and an old soccer ball. I didn't know the president played soccer."

"He's actually a pretty good goalie," said Captain Fact. "But that's not a soccer ball—it's a hornet's nest!"

Captain Fact barely managed to pull the Insectopod around before an angry swarm of hornets came flying out of the nest.

"Hit the turbo boost, Knowledge," ordered Captain Fact. "We've got to get out of here—now!"

As Captain Fact tried to evade the onrushing hornets, his ears began to throb and he felt the start of another . . .

"They're catching up to us," Knowledge gasped, looking over his shoulder. "We're done for!"

"Not yet, my four-legged friend," said Captain Fact calmly. "**KER-FACT!** If you're ever attacked by a swarm of wasps or hornets, you should seek cover in some water and remain submerged until they've passed by!"

Luckily, at that very moment, Captain Fact spotted a pond. He turned the Insectopod in the right direction, and, just in time, the Insectopod splashed into the presidential pond.

CHAPTER 5
POND LIFE

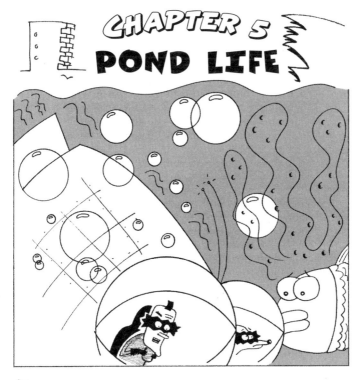

As the Insectopod slipped safely beneath the surface of the pond, the angry hornets gave up their chase and returned to their nest.

"Although hornets do have a really nasty sting, the symptoms don't match the president's," said Captain Fact. "While we're down here, we'd better investigate this pond."

The Insectopod plunged deeper into the murky water. Captain Fact scanned the scene in search of the possible presidential pest. The pond was full of watery creepy-crawlies.

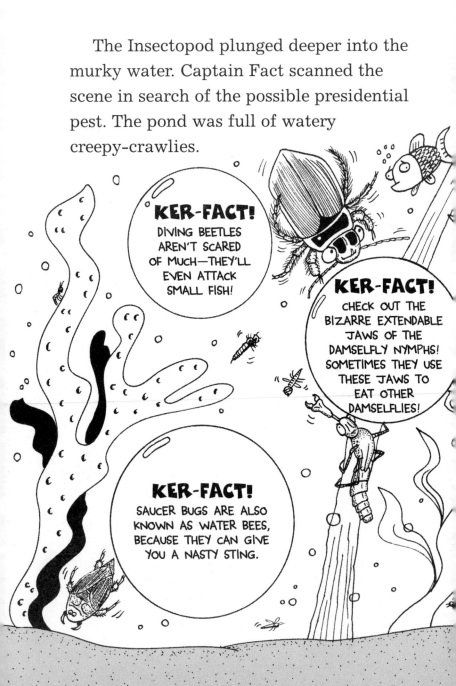

KER-FACT!
DIVING BEETLES AREN'T SCARED OF MUCH—THEY'LL EVEN ATTACK SMALL FISH!

KER-FACT!
CHECK OUT THE BIZARRE EXTENDABLE JAWS OF THE DAMSELFLY NYMPHS! SOMETIMES THEY USE THESE JAWS TO EAT OTHER DAMSELFLIES!

KER-FACT!
SAUCER BUGS ARE ALSO KNOWN AS WATER BEES, BECAUSE THEY CAN GIVE YOU A NASTY STING.

"Well, I don't think we're going to find our bug here, Knowledge. Time to head back to the surface," Captain Fact said. He gripped the steering column tightly, leaned back, and slowly the Insectopod began to ascend from the murky depths.

"Why are we moving so slowly?" asked Knowledge. "It feels like there's an extra passenger on board."

"You're right, Knowledge. We *do* have an extra passenger," said Captain Fact, looking out of the Insectopod worriedly. "It's a bloodsucking leech! And he's trying to suck us out! Reverse thrusters to maximum!" But the harder the Insectopod struggled to pull away, the tighter the leech clamped on.

"How can we get rid of it?" asked Knowledge.

"**KER-FACT!** The best way to remove leeches is by using insect repellent or lemon juice," said Captain Fact, reaching into his lunch bag. "Luckily, lemonade is my favorite." And with that he emptied his lemonade into the torpedo tubes and fired!

The leech released the Insectopod when it got a stinging squirt of lemonade right in the eye.

"Phew," gasped Knowledge as they surfaced and gently bobbed in the waves. "That was a close one!"

Just then, they heard a high-pitched drone. . . .

"Sounds like mosquitoes," said Captain Fact as his elbows began to itch and he launched into a . . .

BURGER

with every meal

IT'S SQUITO-TASTIC!

BUM-IN-A-BUN

FACT

MOSQUITOES HAVE A LARGE, TUBULAR PROBOSCIS (OR NOSE) THAT THEY STICK IN YOU TO SUCK YOUR BLOOD. (YUCK!)

FRENCH FINGERS

FACT

ONLY FEMALE MOSQUITOES BITE— THEY NEED THE BLOOD FOR THEIR EGGS.

LET-O-FOOT

FACT

ALTHOUGH MOSQUITO BITES AREN'T FATAL, THE GERMS THEY CARRY CAN BE. MOSQUITOES HELP SPREAD DISEASES LIKE YELLOW FEVER AND MALARIA.

"Gross!" said Knowledge.

"I agree. And, even worse, mosquitoes aren't what we're looking for," said Captain Fact. Just then, the intercom sparked into life.

UPDATE ON THE PRESIDENT— HE NOW THINKS HE'S A PAIR OF SOCKS AND IS LYING IN THE BOTTOM DRAWER OF HIS DRESSER—*FIZZ*—BUT I'VE JUST LEARNED THAT HE HAD A WORKING BREAKFAST WITH THE SUDANESE AMBASSADOR—*FIZZ*—THE CREEPY-CRAWLY RESPONSIBLE MAY HAVE ACCIDENTALLY BEEN CARRIED IN BY THE AMBASSADOR—*CRACKLE*— YOU'LL NEED TO INVESTIGATE THE SAHARA DESERT— *WHIRR*—TIME TO MAKE THE SEARCH GLOBAL!

CHAPTER 6

THAT STING THING

With the boosters set to supersonic levels, the Insectopod buzzed over land and sea. Finally, the Sahara Desert lay below them.

"It's huge!" gasped Knowledge. As far as he could see was sand.

"**KER-FACT!** The Sahara Desert is the world's biggest desert. Some parts of the desert don't get rain for years!" said Captain Fact.

Captain Fact spotted a good place to land. As they climbed out of the Insectopod, Captain Fact and Knowledge nervously surveyed the dry landscape.

"It's hot out here," said Knowledge, wiping sweat from his brow. "No creepy-crawly could survive in this heat, right?"

"That's where you're wrong," said Captain Fact as something stirred in the sand at his feet. Then a small head popped up and eyes stared at the superheroes.

"Look. It's a baby creepy-crawly," said Knowledge. "He seems lost. Come to Knowledge, little guy. Knowledge has a snack for you."

"I wouldn't do that, Knowledge," Captain Fact warned.

"Why not?" asked Knowledge. "He's cute."

"Because he's a baby scorpion," said Captain Fact, "and they happen to live on their mothers' backs."

Just as he finished his warning, the ground began to shudder and shake.

"He doesn't look so cute now," Knowledge said.

The ground erupted, and there, staring at them angrily, was a huge scorpion. It was the mom—and she was not happy.

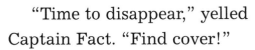

"Time to disappear," yelled Captain Fact. "Find cover!"

As Captain Fact and Knowledge found refuge in a warm pile of mud, Captain Fact's nose began to twitch, and he prepared himself for a . . .

"I don't understand," said Knowledge. "That scorpion didn't come anywhere near us."

"Is it just me, or does something smell funny in here?" interrupted Captain Fact. Just then, the two superheroes began to shudder.

"We're moving!" shrieked Knowledge. They were being pushed along by a large, shiny beetle.

"**KER-FACT!** It's a dung beetle! They live on camel and goat droppings," exclaimed Captain Fact, "which means . . ."

"We jumped into a lump of poo!" said Knowledge. "*Eww!* Let's get out of here!"

Just as they finished extracting themselves from the lump of dung, the sky got dark.

"I thought deserts were dry places," said Knowledge. "It looks like it's going to rain."

"That's not a rain cloud," explained Captain Fact. "It's a swarm of desert locusts! I told you there were lots of creepy-crawlies out here. We have to get back to the Insectopod."

As they sprinted back, Captain Fact's forehead began to throb, and he knew it was time for a . . .

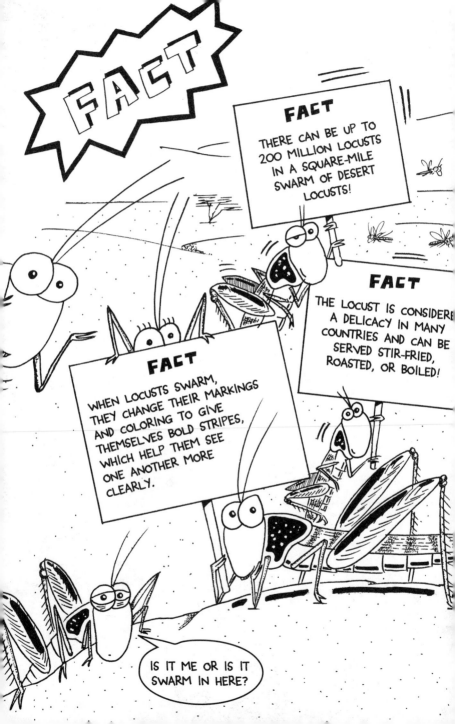

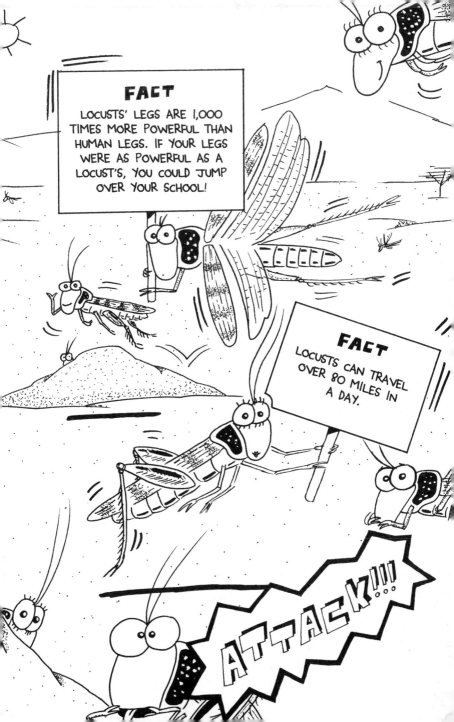

"Locusts are crazy insects! You wouldn't want them coming to a picnic," said Knowledge. He was glad to be inside the Insectopod's cockpit.

Once again, the intercom spluttered to life, and the professor's voice filled the machine.

"This is a presidential update—the president has now dressed up as Little Bo Peep and is discussing world politics with a toaster—*crackle*—I've also just found out that the president and the Brazilian ambassador meet once a week to play soccer—*fizz*—they met this morning and the ambassador had just gotten back from a trip to Brazil—*pop*—head for the Amazonian rain forest at once to check for potential creepy-crawlies."

CHAPTER 7

RUMBLE IN THE JUNGLE!

In no time, Captain Fact and Knowledge were buzzing over the Amazon rain forest in the Insectopod.

"Well, Knowledge, if you think we've met some amazing creepy-crawlies so far, just you wait," Captain Fact said.

"**KER-FACT!** Over half the animal and plant species found on earth live in rain forests." Captain Fact scanned the forest floor for a suitable place to land.

"There," said Knowledge, "a soft, fluffy, landing spot."

"Perfect," said Captain Fact as he landed. "And here, take this umbrella."

As they got out of the Insectopod, it felt as if the ground were moving.

"That's interesting," said Knowledge. "I didn't know there was a bus service. Or that buses had hair!"

"That's because it's not a bus—it's a tarantula!" explained Captain Fact. "But

don't worry. There's no need to panic.
KER-FACT! A tarantula's diet is made up
of insects, frogs, lizards, and mice, and
they can go without food for months at a
time."

"I still don't like the look of those
fangs," said Knowledge. He looked at their
ride's sharp teeth.

"They're used to paralyze prey," said
Captain Fact. "While it's not very pleasant,
the venom is not enough to have harmed
the president."

Suddenly, the tarantula stopped.

"I guess this is the end of our ride," said Captain Fact. "Let's go and see what else is out here."

All around them, jungle creatures scurried and fluttered.

"This place is full of creepy-crawlies," said Knowledge. "Our villain has to be here."

Just then, a giant millipede poked his head out from behind a half-eaten leaf.

"Quick, open up that umbrella!" shouted Captain Fact.

"But it's not raining," Knowledge replied, looking up at the sky.

"Just do it!"

As Knowledge opened the umbrella, the millipede showered them with a fine venomous spray.

Before Captain Fact could explain the effects of millipede venom, he and Knowledge were swept off their feet and carried quickly across the forest floor—by ants!

All around them, millions of ants were grabbing at anything in their path that looked edible . . . including the two superheroes!

Despite being on his back, and firmly in the grip of a serious-looking worker ant, Captain Fact's chin began to throb as he launched into a . . .

The ants kept marching, and finally, Captain Fact and Knowledge were carried deep into the ants' nest.

"It looks like we're home delivery for an ant colony," Captain Fact said. "Ant grubs have insatiable appetites."

"So that makes us grub grub," gulped Knowledge, trying to lighten the mood.

All of a sudden, the ants seemed to panic. They began dropping everything and running all over the place. A long, thin, wiggly tongue was waggling above them. The Insectopod was already stuck to it!

"Quick, this is our chance to escape—it's a giant anteater!" Captain Fact said excitedly. "Jump on its tongue!"

"I'm not going anywhere near that slimy thing," said Knowledge.

"Would you rather be ant dinner?" asked Captain Fact as he grabbed Knowledge and leaped aboard the sticky tongue. With an almighty slurp, they were sucked up and out of the nest by the hungry anteater.

Just as Captain Fact had hoped,
the anteater didn't like the idea of
a superhero snack and
quickly spat the two
out.

Wet and sticky but otherwise unharmed,
Captain Fact and Knowledge gratefully got
into the Insectopod. They had had just
about enough of the rain forest.

CHAPTER 8

BLUNDER DOWN UNDER

As the superheroes cleaned themselves off, the intercom spluttered again.

"Come in, Insectopod—*crackle*—come in, Insectopod—there's been a change of plan—*fizz*—I've just discovered that the president was guest of honor at a lunch hosted by the Australian prime minister—*pop*—you must proceed at once to Australia—*fizz . . .*"

Taking one last look at the buggy jungle, Captain Fact and Knowledge blasted off to the land "down under."

A little while later, the Insectopod touched down in Australia, barely avoiding being trampled by a mob of kangaroos.

"**KER-FACT!** Australia is the world's biggest island continent and home to nearly a quarter of a million types of creepy-crawly," said Captain Fact as he got out of the Insectopod, "so we have to make sure we don't waste time tangling with the wrong bug."

"I think it might be too late. Looks like I'm already tangled up in something," said Knowledge, looking down at his paws.

Before they could figure out what was happening, the two superheroes had been swept up by some big, hairy legs and placed in a hole.

"I've heard that Australians were friendly," said Knowledge, "but this is amazing! Two complete strangers, and we're literally dragged in for a visit!"

"Unfortunately, Knowledge, your new best friend is actually a trap-door spider, and we're his afternoon snack," whispered Captain Fact. He peered through the gloom and realized there was no way out.

"Does this mean what I think it means?" asked Knowledge.

"It certainly does, Knowledge," Captain Fact said, pressing the emergency button on his Fact Watch.

Almost instantly there was a commotion at the entrance of the trap-door spider's hole.

"It looks like some kind of beetle," said Captain Fact. "Let's hope the spider finds it more appealing than us."

Sure enough, the trap-door spider glanced over its shoulder, saw the invader, and eagerly set off to grab the tasty morsel.

"Quick, Knowledge, here's our chance. Let's go for it," said Captain Fact, grabbing Knowledge and making a run for freedom.

Outside, the beetle was running rings around the spider. It bounced and flew beyond the reach of the spider's eight hairy legs.

"I didn't know there were beetle species made out of metal," said Knowledge, "with flowery patterns."

"That's not a beetle. It's Factorella!" Captain Fact said.

"Hello, you two! Isn't this fun?" shouted Factorella. "Dad just finished building the Beetlebuggy this morning!"

"It's the first time I've ever been happy to see a creepy-crawly," said Knowledge. "I didn't think they could be useful!"

"Actually, Knowledge, only a tiny
number of bugs are real nuisances," said
Captain Fact. "And a lot of them are really
very useful." His shins began to shudder
and his head pounded as he felt the
beginning of another . . .

Factorella's zigzaggy flying had left the trap-door spider so dizzy that it was now lying on its back with its head spinning.

Factorella turned to Captain Fact and Knowledge. "You need to find our villainous creepy-crawly quickly," she said. "The president now thinks he's King Kong and is on the roof swiping at pigeons. I'd love to help, but I've got to get back."

And with that, the Beetlebuggy disappeared over the horizon.

The adventurous pair got back on the Insectopod. "It's now or never, Knowledge," said Captain Fact. "I've got one last idea where the creepy-crawly might be hiding." With that, the Insectopod was off.

CHAPTER 9
BIT ON THE BUTT!

As the Insectopod landed in the Australian prime minister's home, Captain Fact knew there was no time to waste.

"We're heading straight for the bathroom!" Captain Fact said.

"Great idea," said Knowledge. "A long, hot bath would be great after a day of bug hunting. I do feel quite dirty. Did you bring bubble bath?"

But Captain Fact wasn't listening to Knowledge. He was boldly going where no man had gone before: into the darkness behind the prime minister's toilet.

"Our creepy-crawly has got to be here somewhere," he said. "Knowledge, you investigate the actual bowl. I'm going to check out the . . . Knowledge?" But Knowledge was nowhere to be seen.

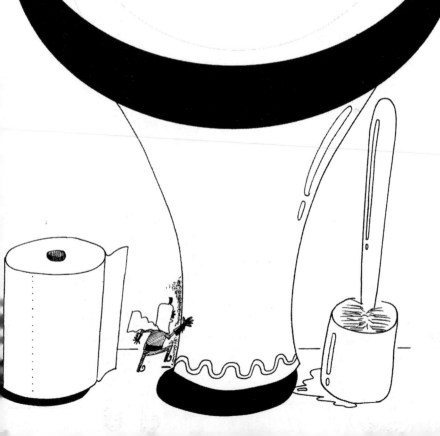

Then, all of a sudden, Knowledge came bounding back into view.

"Captain Fact, look, I'm an airplane . . . wheeeee, wheeeee. Your cape looks like a giant banana. I like banana splits. Can I have a bite, please? Please?"

"Knowledge, what happened to you?" asked Captain Fact as his normally well-behaved sidekick started doing handstands while reciting doggy poetry.

BOW-WOW-WOW! YOU SMELL LIKE A COW.

"I just got bitten by a spider," said Knowledge as he licked Captain Fact's hair. "It was a little painful at first, but now I just feel strange."

"Where were you bitten?" asked Captain Fact frantically.

"On my bottom, if you must know," replied Knowledge, a bit embarrassed.

"No. I meant, where in the bathroom?"

"Over there—by that funnel-shaped web," said Knowledge.

"Knowledge! You've done it!" shouted Captain Fact. "Your bottom has just saved the president! We have to get back to the Insectopod at once!"

Captain Fact picked up Knowledge, who was now lying on his back, demanding to be tickled, and sprinted to the Insectopod.

Once there, he immediately contacted the Fact Cave. "Come in, Professor Minuscule! Come in, Professor Minuscule!"

"Minuscule here. I hear you loud and clear," the professor replied.

"We've got our bug," said Captain Fact. "Well, actually, Knowledge got it. I mean—"

"I don't care who's got it or how you got it. Just tell me what it is!" demanded Professor Minuscule.

Captain Fact cleared his throat dramatically. "It's a Sydney funnel-web spider! That's what bit the president!" he announced proudly. "**KER-FACT!** Its venom attacks the nerves of the body, causing muscle twitches, perspiration, and tears. It also causes changes in blood vessels, which can affect the brain, leading to shock. This explains the president's strange behavior."

"Of course!—*fizz*—one of the world's most deadly arthropods—*crackle*—fortunately, an antivenom for the Sydney funnel-web spider has been around since 1980—*crackle*—I'll inform the presidential doctors at once—*wobble*—you've done it!—*crackle*—you've saved the day!"

"What should I do about Knowledge?" asked Captain Fact anxiously.

"Oh, there's some antivenom in the Insectopod first-aid kit—*fizz*—an injection of that will fix him right up."

As Captain Fact administered the antivenom, his head began to wobble, and he was struck by another . . .

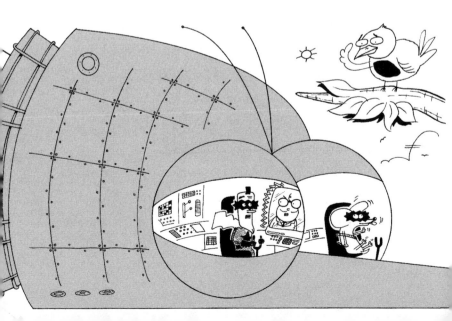

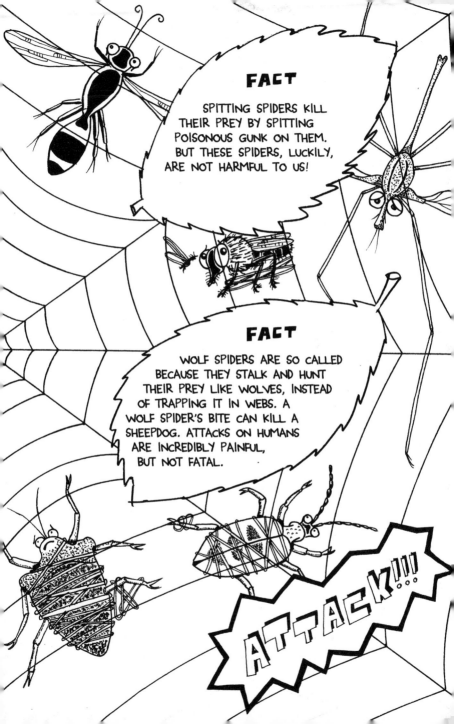

Captain Fact gave Knowledge the antivenom shot and waited.

Slowly Knowledge began to come around.

"I feel much better. Where am I? Recuperating on one of Australia's stunning beaches? Being looked after by the world's leading spider-bite experts?"

"Are you sure you're feeling better? You still sound delusional, Knowledge. You're in the Insectopod with me. We're heading home, so get changed. We've got the evening weather to do!"

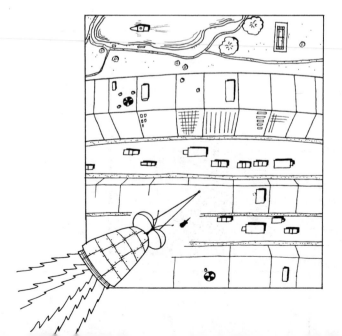

CHAPTER 10

AND NOW, THE WEATHER . . .

"**C**ome in, Insectopod—*crackle*—as soon as you're back in your office—*fizz*—you'll eject—*crackle*—then I'll unshrink you, using the remote control!" said Professor Minuscule.

"That sounds perfect," replied Captain Fact, who was back in Cliff form, as he targeted his office window. "What can go wrong now?"

Just then a huge gust of wind (that Cliff hadn't forecast) swept them into the wrong office. Right into—the Boss's office!

"Professor Minuscule!" squeaked Cliff. "Don't unshrink us . . ."

But it was too late. There was a pulse of light and a blue flash, and Cliff and Puddles found themselves sitting in the Boss's lap.

"I must have sunstroke," said the Boss, looking very dazed and confused as Cliff and Puddles dashed out of his office. "I knew I should have had more shade inside my tent."

Breathlessly, Cliff and Puddles burst into the Makeup department.

"There you two are," said Lucy when she saw them. "Have you heard the news?"

"No, what happened?" asked Cliff.

"The president's been saved!" said Lucy. "If Captain Fact hadn't saved the day, they might never have figured out what bit him. He got the serum just in time. I'd love to catch Captain Fact in *my* web. . . ."

Cliff blushed as Puddles led him into the studio.

And so, with the president safely back at his desk running the country, Cliff Thornhill and Puddles went safely back to doing what they did worst—the weather.

Until the next crisis . . .

KNIFE AND PACKER'S SCARIEST CREEPY-CRAWLY ENCOUNTER WAS WHEN A HUMONGOUS WASP SNUCK IN THROUGH THE OFFICE WINDOW ONE SUMMER. IT MOVED INTO THEIR ONE AND ONLY PENCIL CASE, AND THEY WERE FORCED TO WORK IN THE BATHROOM!